MW00902068

Clara & Layla:
The Great Investigators
The Purple Shoe and the Frooglebum Cave

ISBN-13: 978-1544661520
ISBN-10: 1544661525

DADDY'S BUTTERFLY
(Layla)

DADDY'S BIRD
(Clara)

CLARA & LAYLA
JAXONPHOTOGROUP.COM

Dedication:

To My Bird and My Butterfly...
It is in the tint of your skin, the curl of
your hair and the glow of your smile...
It is an everlasting strength and beauty and
it will be yours for all time...
Always keep your heart...

Daddy Loves You...

In an ordinary house, on an ordinary night,
a mother kissed her daughters' heads
and turned on the night light.

"Good Night Clara, Good Night Layla.
Have sweet dreams and go to sleep."
And as soon as mommy left,
out of bed did Clara sneak.

"Wake up Layla", Clara whispered.
"Hurry, before it's too late.
If we stay asleep much longer,
we will never crack the case."

"I'm awake, I'm awake",
Layla said and stretched and yawned.
"I'm awake."
Then she slid from bed
and put her slippers on.

"Make sure you are very quiet, Layla.
We're going to solve a case.
We are two investigators
and we have no time to waste."

"Take a look there on the closet floor.
There's one of your purple shoes.
The other one's gone missing
and we have to find some clues."

"Where should we start to look for clues?
Where should we start our search?"
As Layla yawned one last time she said,
"Where should we both look first?"

Just then Clara had a thought.
What would make their great quest greater,
is if they had another friend to help,
a third investigator.

She slowly opened up their door
and coming down the hall,
was their third investigator friend,
Roc, the family dog.

"With Roc we'll find it right away.
He's got a super nose.
He'll lead us to your missing shoe
with one sniff of your toes!"

"But first we'll need to make a list
of places we will look.
We'll write them down and check them off
in this red notebook."

"Hey, I know where we should look first!"
said Layla very proudly.
"Sssshhhh Layla! You have to whisper!
You cannot talk so loudly."

"But I..." and just as Layla spoke,
her sister gave a look.
Then Clara opened up the cover
and wrote in her notebook.

"We'll start our search beneath your bed;
a well, so dark and deep.
We'll have to climb down on a rope
where creepy crawlers creep."

"But Clara, I don't see a well,
here underneath my bed.
There's only floor and clothes and toys.
Have you fallen on your head?"

"Layla, there's a well down there,
that's dark and black as night.
But do not worry, not one bit,
for here's a magic light!"

Just at that moment
Layla closed her eyes and squeezed them tight.
And her imagination
helped her see the magic light!

"I see it Clara!" Layla screamed
and smiled from ear to ear.
"Quiet Layla" Clara scolded.
"Do you want a goblin to hear!?"

They climbed down quickly
and reached the bottom.
The well was creepy and damp.
As they walked along a dark smelly hall,
Layla heard a very faint 'pant'.

"Clara Clara, did you hear that noise,
like something is breathing real close?
Maybe it's a bear or a wolf or a dragon.
Maybe it's a monster or ghost!"

As quick as she could, Clara turned with her light,
to shine and see what was there.
And there stood a goblin, but only 3 feet tall
with a red and yellow crown in its hair.

This goblin was not scary at all.
He smiled then said "How do you do?
My name is Von Sugary Van Cloogie the Third,
the GOOblin King... It's nice to meet you!"

"Don't you mean Goblin?" Clara said in a rush,
as she tried to correct what he'd said.
"GOBLIN!? Heavens no, I'm a GOOblin my dear,
that lives underneath your bed."

"We Gooblins are nice and we love children so.
Nothing like our goblin foes.
When you sleep at night, we Gooblins come out
and we love to sniff your toes!"

"Well hello Von Sugary! We're solving a case.
Perhaps you can help with a need.
I'm Clara, she's Layla, and that's our dog Roc,
and we could use your assistance indeed."

"I'd be glad to help! No problem at all!
But I have one request of you two.
Might I have a smell of your wiggly toes?
After all, that's what Gooblins do!"

And as quick as a wink,
he was down on his knees,
to catch a whiff of their feet.
He giggled with joy as he sniffed Layla's toes.
"Aaaahhh, they smell so wonderfully sweet!!!"

After he was done, with a smile on his face,
to his feet, Von Sugary stood.
He began to lead them further into the hall,
just as he said that he would.

16

"I already know what you're searching for.
A purple shoe, is that right?
I was able to hear you talking before
when you mentioned your magic light."

After walking awhile, Von Sugary stopped
at a door that seemed to give him a scare.
Even Roc gave a growl, and a sign was posted,
"STOP!!! Do Not Enter!!! BEWARE!!!"

"I am sorry you both, I can go no further.
We Gooblins don't go in that place.
This door leads straight into
the FroogleBum's Cave
and trust me, it's very unsafe!"

"Well Clara, maybe we should head back that way.
I'm scared of FroogleBums too!"
Then Clara turned to her scared little sis and said,
"What can a FroogleBum do?"

18

"What's a FroogleBum anyway?" she asked their new friend,
and he replied with great concern.
"I've never seen one, but when anyone goes in there,
they never ever return!"

So he bid them farewell and gave them a wink,
and gave Roc a pat on the ear.
And into the dark of the hall to the well,
Von Sugary the Gooblin king, disappeared.

"Clara, I'm scared. I don't want to go
into the cave where the FroogleBum roams.
I think we should go back up in the well.
I think we should all go home!"

"But Layla, you have nothing to fear.
Roc isn't afraid of this cave.
He'll protect us for sure. He won't let us get hurt.
With him we'll both be safe."

Layla looked at their dog
and couldn't believe what happened next,
and didn't know what to think.
Roc stood on two legs and said, "Have no fear!"
and gave them both a wink.

"I'll keep you safe! You are my best friends.
That Frooglebum doesn't scare me!
I'll give him a bark and a whip of my tail.
He won't know what hit him, you'll see!"

Roc kicked open the door and they followed him in
to the cave that was home to the beast.
As they walked further into the Frooglebums cave,
their dog Roc wasn't scared in the least.

BOOM!

Though they couldn't see much
past their small magic light,
they could tell there was something nearby.
Then out of nowhere, what was in front of them,
but a large pair of glowing green eyes.

"Who's there!?" said Roc,
in a loud growling voice.
"Come out! For we are not afraid!"
"Yeah that's right, we're not scared of you",
both girls said, though behind Roc they stayed.

There was quiet a while,
and the eyes kept their stare,
as their green continued to glow.
Then a large orange figure
came out from the shadows,
and stepped into the light slow.

The figure was large and as tall as a horse,
with a tail like the tail of a cat.
It had 2 arms and legs, and on top of it's head,
a crown made of fresh flowers sat.

"Greetings you three. Welcome here to my home.
I am Lolita, the Queen FroogleBum.
You're definitely not Gooblins,
so we're glad you are here
from wherever it is you have come."

"But your signs said 'STOP, DO NOT ENTER, BEWARE!'",
Layla was sure to say.
"Oh yes, but don't worry, we're happy you're here.
That's just to keep Gooblins away."

"But why would you want to keep Gooblins out?
Have you met Von Sugary Van Cloogie the Third?"
Lolita said "I've actually never seen a Gooblin
and that name I've never heard."

"Then how do you know if you like them or not?
You should really give others a try.
It's not nice to dislike those you do not know,
if you have no reason why."

Lolita stopped to think a bit,
about what Clara had said,
and decided, "You know, you're absolutely right.
I'll welcome the Gooblins instead!"

"TO ALL THOSE HERE IN THE FROOGLEBUM CAVE,
HEAR THIS AND HEAR IT WELL.
FROM NOW ON GOOBLINS ARE WELCOME HERE!"
Queen Lolita said in a yell!

Her yell was so loud it shook the whole cave,
and reached the Gooblin well.
Just then Von Sugary Van Cloogie the Third
came running in ringing a bell!

"So happy to hear this! So glad to meet you!
I've brought all my family and friends!
Von Rufus, Von Toofus and Uncle Von Slump
and over there, Cousin Von Chins!"

The Gooblins and Frooglebums danced
and they sang.
Both Clara and Layla joined too.
And after a while they'd almost forgotten
about Layla's lost purple shoe.

"Layla and Clara!" Roc called aloud.
"Don't forget why we're here in this place.
This party is wonderfully fun, yes indeed,
but we are still solving a case!"

"Yes you are right! We must find the shoe!
Lolita can you help us please?"
"You've come a long way,
down the well, down the hall
and I'll surely help you with ease!"

At the top of that hill is a big bright blue door.
Go through it and find what you seek.
The Gooblins and Frooglebums hate to see you go,
but thank you for bringing us peace!"

Roc and the girls traveled on to the hill,
while waving to all their new friends.
To the top of the hill, to the big bright blue door,
they were ready to finally go in.

With a turn of the knob, Clara pulled the door open.
There shined a very bright light.
And once it got dim enough for their eyes,
they noticed a very odd sight.

As they looked around it was plain to see
that after they came into the doors...
Why, they ended up right back in their room
and Roc was back on all fours.

"But I don't understand, the Queen said she'd help.
She said we would find it for sure.
She said the shoe was up the hill,
and just behind the door."

Clara sat, very puzzled and could not understand
where the shoe was she thought they would find.
And just then Layla said, "But Clara, she was right!
The shoe was here the whole time!"

"Remember just before we went to the well,
I wanted to look some place other?
If you would have listened to what I was saying,
I'd have told you...
THE SHOE IS UNDER MY COVERS!"

They laughed and they laughed
and they talked all about it; the well, the cave and all.
Then they jumped into their beds
as quick as they could,
when they heard daddy coming down the hall.

Dad peeked in their room to make sure they were ok.
They didn't move or make a peep.
With their eyes closed and a smile on their face,
Layla and Clara both went to sleep.

JAXON PHOTO GROUP

"The Purple Shoe and the Frooglebum Cave" is the first title from the "Clara & Layla: The Great Investigators" Series from author, Moses A. Hardie, III. Residing in Atlanta, Georgia, Moses is a graduate of Hampton University (Class of 2004 - B.S. Business Management). The main characters of the series are his two beautiful daughters, Clara and Layla. "My main goal for the series was to have not only my two girls, but kids everywhere be able to pick up a book and see faces that look like their own. Their only limit is their imagination and I want theirs to be endless."

Illustrator Sean L. Miller is a Norfolk, Virginia native who is an award-winning Graphic Designer, Marketing Specialist, and Educator. He received his Bachelor of Fine Arts from Old Dominion University, Master of Arts in Religious Studies from Howard University, and Master in Education from Regent University. One of Sean's goals is to establish visual and performance arts centers throughout the United States that will serve as platforms where artists will have a venue to express themselves.

The vision of Sean L. Miller's personal ministry is to identify God's will and apply it to the artistic abilities of individuals, therefore developing a network of Christ-centered visual artists and musicians who create in an effort to glorify God and uplift communities.

76729978R00024

Made in the USA
Columbia, SC
09 September 2017